Aladdin
— AND THE —
Magic Lamp

A Parragon Book

Published by
Parragon Books,
Unit 13-17, Avonbridge Trading Estate,
Atlantic Road, Avonmouth, Bristol BS11 9QD

Produced by
The Templar Company plc,
Pippbrook Mill, London Road, Dorking, Surrey RH4 1JE

Designed by Mark Kingsley-Monks

Printed and bound in Italy

ISBN 0-75250-788-5

Aladdin
── AND THE ──
Magic Lamp

Retold by Caroline Repchuk
Illustrated by Helen Cockburn

‖ •PARRAGON• ‖

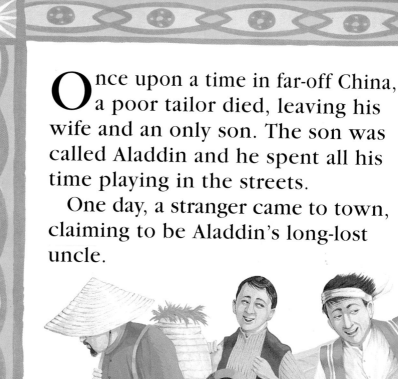

Once upon a time in far-off China, a poor tailor died, leaving his wife and an only son. The son was called Aladdin and he spent all his time playing in the streets.

One day, a stranger came to town, claiming to be Aladdin's long-lost uncle.

Little did Aladdin realise that the stranger was really a cunning magician who needed help to carry out a wicked plan. Over supper, Aladdin's mother begged the uncle to find work for her son and he gladly agreed, saying, "Tomorrow he can work for me!"

The next day the magician took Aladdin for a long walk outside the city gates. When they reached a particular spot, he suggested they stop for a rest and a morsel of cake. Then, while Aladdin's back was turned, the magician muttered a

magic spell which caused the earth to split open, revealing a stone with a brass ring in it.

"Beneath here is a treasure which will be yours if you do as I say," said the wicked man and he bade the amazed Aladdin to lift the great stone.

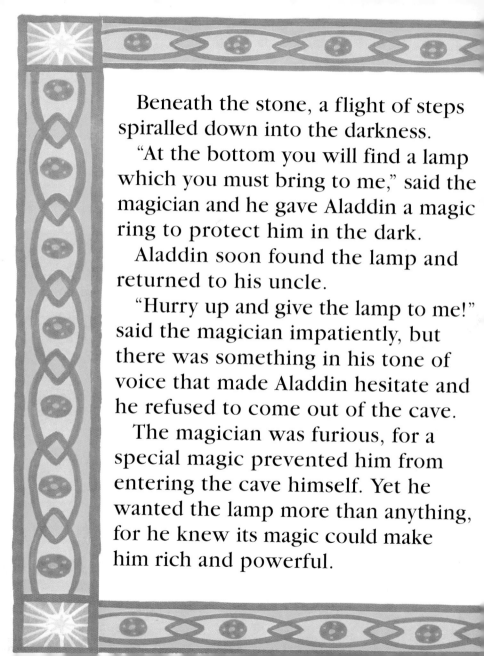

Beneath the stone, a flight of steps spiralled down into the darkness.

"At the bottom you will find a lamp which you must bring to me," said the magician and he gave Aladdin a magic ring to protect him in the dark.

Aladdin soon found the lamp and returned to his uncle.

"Hurry up and give the lamp to me!" said the magician impatiently, but there was something in his tone of voice that made Aladdin hesitate and he refused to come out of the cave.

The magician was furious, for a special magic prevented him from entering the cave himself. Yet he wanted the lamp more than anything, for he knew its magic could make him rich and powerful.

Cursing in rage, the magician threw more powder on the steps and the stone rolled back into place! Then he fled, leaving Aladdin trapped in the cave.

Poor Aladdin sat weeping and, as he did so, he accidentally rubbed the magic ring. With a great puff of smoke, a huge genie appeared.

"What is your wish?" thundered the genie. "I am the Slave of the Ring and will obey you."

Aladdin begged, "Free me from this place!" At once he found himself outside and ran home to his mother as fast as he could to tell her what had happened.

As Aladdin was telling her his story, his mother started absent-mindedly polishing the old lamp. Suddenly, there was a huge flash, and a great genie appeared before them, saying:

"I am the Genie of the Lamp and will grant your every wish!"

Now Aladdin was delighted by this strange turn of events, for he had fallen in love with the Sultan's beautiful daughter. Perhaps the Genie could help him win her hand in marriage?

So Aladdin asked the Genie for a bag of precious jewels and then bade his mother visit the Sultan with them.

Now Aladdin's mother did just as he asked, and went to see the Sultan who was amazed at the sight of the precious jewels. But his chief adviser, the Grand Vizir, was not pleased. He wanted the Princess to marry his own son and so he persuaded the Sultan to wait three months before giving Aladdin permission to marry. In that time, he was sure that his son could find a more valuable gift.

Sure enough, two months later Aladdin's mother went to town and found everyone rejoicing. The Vizir's son was to marry the Princess that very night!

She ran and told Aladdin, who
summoned the Genie of the Lamp
and ordered him to fetch the couple.

"Lock him up," ordered Aladdin,
pointing to the Vizir's son, when
they arrived. Alone with the
Princess he gently explained
that she had first been
promised to him.

Next morning, the Genie
took the frightened pair
back to the Palace.

The angry Sultan demanded to know where they had been, and reluctantly they told him what had happened. By now, the Vizir's son was terrified, and begged for the wedding to be cancelled.

After three months, Aladdin sent his mother to remind the Sultan of his promise. This time the Vizir advised him to ask a far higher price than Aladdin could afford.

So the Sultan declared, "I will keep my promise if your son sends me forty golden bowls filled with jewels, carried by forty fine slaves."

Aladdin's mother sadly went home, thinking that all was lost.

But Aladdin summoned the Genie, and soon slaves with bowls of gems were marching through the Palace gates. The Sultan was astonished and gave Aladdin his blessing at once.

Aladdin began preparing for the wedding and again he called on the Genie of the Lamp.

"I want some fine silk clothes, a magnificent horse and ten thousand pieces of gold in ten purses," he said, and it was no sooner said than done. "Now to build a marble Palace fit for the Princess," Aladdin continued. "It must have walls of gold and silver, set with precious stones. See to it at once!"

Aladdin's splendid Palace was finished the very next day, and everyone was astounded by it. Soon it was time for the wedding.

The Princess was delighted to be marrying Aladdin, for she thought him the most handsome man she had ever seen. She happily obeyed her father and the marriage took place with much rejoicing.

Aladdin soon won the hearts of the people. He was made Captain of the Sultan's army and did many good deeds throughout the land. And so Aladdin and his Princess lived happily for several years.

But far away in Africa the evil magician had discovered that Aladdin had married a Princess, and was living in splendour. He knew it must be the work of the lamp, and he decided to win it back.

He travelled night and day until he reached the city, where he heard talk of Prince Aladdin's marvellous palace. "That lamp will be mine!" he raged, "and Aladdin will live in poverty once more."

The evil magician waited until Aladdin was away from home. Then he disguised himself as a merchant and knocked on the Palace door, offering to sell new lamps for old.

The unsuspecting Princess was only too happy to get rid of Aladdin's old lamp, little realising its true worth.

The magician snatched it and hurried away, busily plotting his revenge.

Next morning the Sultan looked out of the window and rubbed his eyes, for Aladdin's Palace was gone! The magician had ordered the Genie to carry it and the princess back to his home in Africa.

The Sultan sent at once for the Grand Vizir who declared that Aladdin must be an evil sorcerer, and when Aladdin called at the palace on his way home, he found the Sultan waiting for him in a fury.

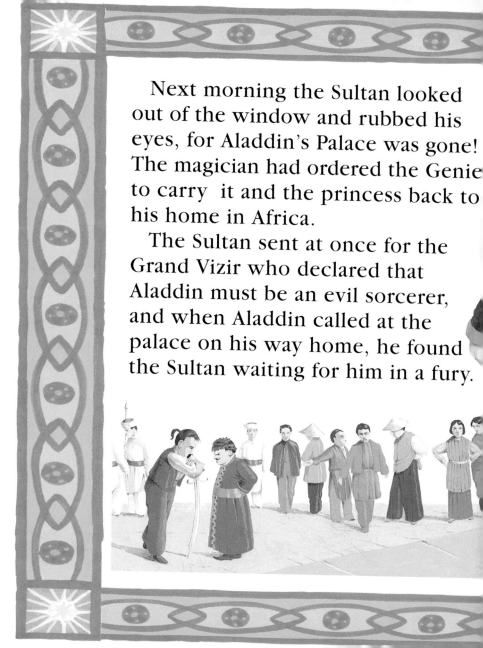

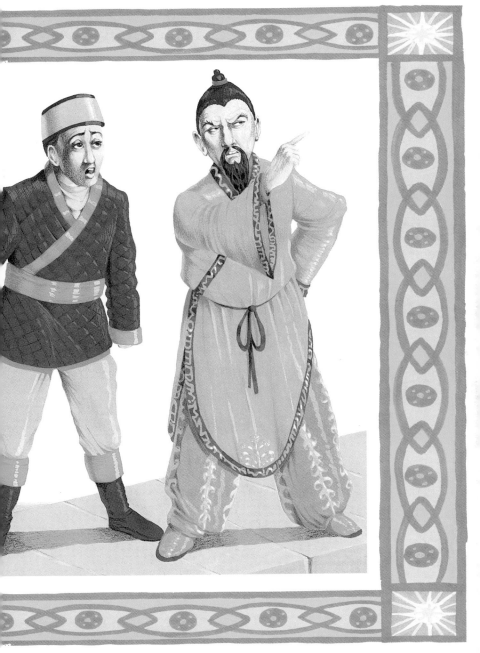

The Sultan demanded to know where his daughter was, and gave Aladdin forty days to find her. If he failed he would be executed.

Aladdin was heartbroken and wept bitterly. But as he clasped his hands he rubbed the magic ring on his finger. Instantly, the Genie of the Ring appeared, saying "What is your wish, oh, master?"

"Save my life, Genie," he said, "and bring my Palace back."

"That is not in my power," said the Genie. "Ask the Genie of the Lamp."

"Very well then," said Aladdin, "Take me to the Palace instead." Now, far away in Africa the magician was busy trying to woo the Princess. He kept her locked in her room and visited her every day, but she dreaded his visits and would not speak to him.

You can imagine her joy when she opened her window and found Aladdin asleep on the ledge outside! Aladdin asked at once what had become of his old lamp, and soon he understood that the Genie of the Lamp had a new master!

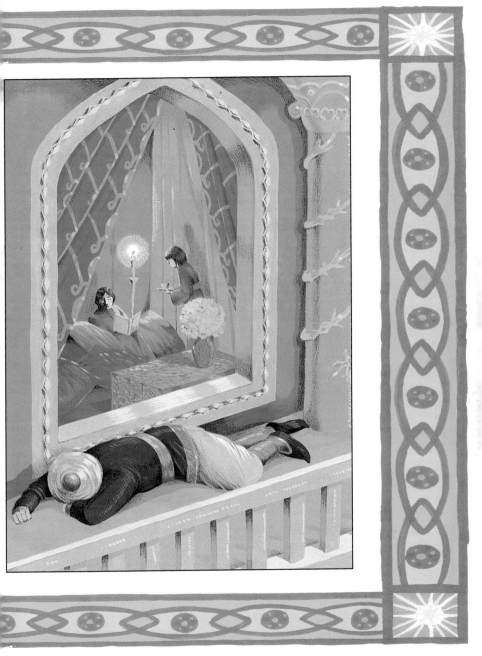

Aladdin had soon devised a clever plan to retrieve his lamp, for he guessed that it had been stolen by his evil "uncle".

"Invite him to dine with you," he told her, "and when he arrives, this is what you must do."

She listened carefully and, that evening, asked the delighted magician to visit her and drink her health, exchanging glasses as a sign of friendship. Little did he know that she had put some powder Aladdin had given her into her glass.

She watched as the magician drank every drop. His eyes widened in horror and he clutched at his throat. "I've been poisoned!" he gasped and fell lifeless to the floor.

Aladdin sprung out from behind a curtain, took the lamp from the dead magician's robe and ordered the Genie to carry the Palace and all inside back to China once more.

The Sultan was overjoyed to find his daughter safe and well and the Palace back in its original place. He turned to Aladdin, who explained what had happened.

"An evil magician spirited away your daughter but now he is dead and we can all live in peace again."

After this Aladdin and his wife did indeed live in peace in their beautiful Palace. And, when the Sultan died, Aladdin took his place and reigned for many happy years.

Aladdin belongs to one of the greatest story collections of all time: *The Tales of the Arabian Nights.* These stories were first heard many hundreds of years ago and include *The Voyages of Sinbad the Sailor* and *The Magic Carpet.*
First translated into French by Antoine Galland at the beginning of the 18th century, they were originally told by the beautiful Princess Scheherezade to the suspicious Prince of Tartary, who had threatened to behead her at daybreak. But her tales were so exciting that, as the sun rose, he longed to hear how they ended and so pardoned her life for one more day, until after one thousand and one nights Scheherezade had won his trust and his heart.